GRANDMOTHER BRYANT'S POCKET

GRANDMOTHER ❧❧❧ BRYANT'S ❧❧❧ ❧❧❧❧ POCKET ❧❧❧❧

by JACQUELINE BRIGGS MARTIN

pictures by PETRA MATHERS

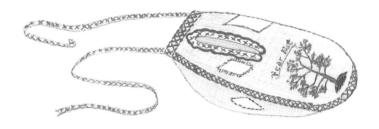

HOUGHTON MIFFLIN COMPANY

Boston 1996

Manufactured in the United States of America

Book design by David Saylor
The text of this book is set in 14-point Monotype Fournier.
The illustrations are watercolor, reproduced in full color.

WOZ 10 9 8 7 6 5 4 3 2 1

LIBRARY OF CONGRESS CATALOGING-IN-PUBLICATION DATA
Martin, Jacqueline Briggs.
Grandmother Bryant's pocket / by Jacqueline Briggs Martin ;
illustrated by Petra Mathers. p. cm.
Summary: Suffering from nightmares after her dog is killed in a fire,
a young girl in 18th-century Maine goes to live with her grandparents.
ISBN 0-395-68984-8
[1. Fear—Fiction. 2. Nightmares—Fiction. 3. Grandparents—Fiction.
4. Maine—Fiction.] I. Mathers, Petra, ill. II. Title.
PZ7.M363165Gr   1996
[E]—dc20   94-31309   CIP   AC

For my grandmothers and grandfathers;
for Justin and Sarah's
grandmothers and grandfathers

J. B. M.

For my family in New Haven

P. M.

A Note About Pockets

HUNDREDS OF YEARS AGO, pockets were not sewn into skirts as they are now. Although a man's breeches had sewn-in pockets, a woman tied a pocket around her waist, under her skirt. Slits in the skirt allowed her to reach it. A woman's pocket contained useful items she might need as she did her daily work. It might also contain a coin or a gold button.

❧ Sarah Bryant

SARAH BRYANT was eight years old in 1787.
She lived on a farm in Maine
and had a spotted dog called Patches.
Every day Patches waited while Sarah churned butter,
gathered the eggs, or fed the pig.

Sometimes they went to the field behind the barn
to run, climb on boulders too big for men to move,
or lie on the grass and listen to robins.

When Sarah talked to Patches
she thought he understood,
and she was never afraid
when they walked down the road together.

Sarah Bryant's Dreams

IN EARLY spring the barn burned down,
and Patches was caught in the fire.
Then Sarah dreamed of fire and smoke.
Her mother gave her hot milk at night.
Her father gave her the best quilt.
They moved her featherbed out of the loft
and laid it beside their own bed.

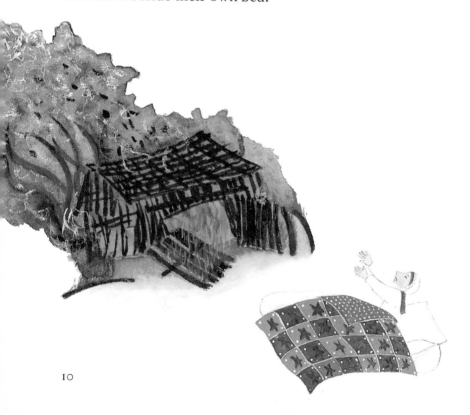

But the dreams stuck to her skin
like the smell of soot,
and she woke up calling for Patches.
Finally her father said,
"Your grandparents want you to stay
some time with them—away from these ashes.
Grandmother Bryant knows about roots and plants.
Maybe she will know a cure for your bad dreams."

❧ Grandmother Bryant

GRANDMOTHER BRYANT was quiet and strong.
She hung herbs to dry from kitchen beams.
She carried chamomile, knitbone, and pennyroyal
in her pocket to cure aches and scrapes and colds.

Day or night, people came to her
to ask for help with birthing babies,
burns and chills, cuts and sores,
and they paid her in bacon, linen, salt, or coins.

Grandmother Bryant was steady and sure.
She knew the medicines that grew in woods and gardens.
She hoped she could find a cure for nighttime fears.

⸙ Grandfather Bryant's Stories

GRANDFATHER BRYANT made buckets and barrels.
He whittled trinkets and toys from scraps of wood.
Everyone called him Shoe Peg
and they waited for his stories.

He told of his mother—such a good knitter,
she knitted a mitten underwater
the day she fell off the Kennebec ferryboat.
He told of biscuits he ate in Boston—
so hard they had to be soaked in sea water
and run over by a wagon wheel before he could chew them.
His voice was loud. His songs were booming.
But he could catch butterflies
without hurting feeler or wing.

✤ The One-Eyed Cat

NO ONE knew where the one-eyed cat had come from.
Sarah said it looked hungry and lost,
afraid of strangers and alone.
Shoe Peg said the cat would bring bad luck.
But Grandmother Bryant said any cat
that could catch mice on the first jump
would keep rats out of the root cellar
and mice out of the bags of wheat in the attic,
and ought to be given a home.
No matter about the one eye and the short tail—
Grandmother Bryant said that cat
would never bring trouble.

❧ The Neighbor

GRANDFATHER SAID Beck Chadwick
would walk uphill to make trouble.
She claimed the plumpest hog from the common field,
though everyone knew the runt was hers.
She kept a cow and sold the milk,
but people said she watered it.
They said she would cut off her mother's hair
for a gold button.
She carried gossip in her pocket and her basket,
and she would rather spread bad words than eat apples.

❧ Beck Chadwick's Geese

BECK CHADWICK's geese were tall and mean
and wouldn't stay at her place.
They'd go after a kitten or a dog,
steal a strawberry, or bite a child.
They nipped and pinched at Sarah's arms.
She had no Patches to make her brave
and she dared not go outside by herself.
The geese could smell her fear
and would chase her across the yard,
hissing and honking.

❦ Not Clowns or Chamomile Tea

SARAH'S DREAMS came into the night like sudden storms.
Grandmother Bryant gave her chamomile tea at bedtime,
but Sarah woke up shaking from dreams of fire.
Shoe Peg carved a dancing clown to sit by the bed,
but Sarah dreamed of Patches and woke up crying.
Shoe Peg said, "There are no quick cures."
He hummed and whittled by Sarah's bed.
Grandmother Bryant wondered if her pocket
might work a cure.

༄ Grandmother Bryant's Pocket

GRANDMOTHER BRYANT held the pocket
while she told Sarah of her long-ago dreams
of falling down a hill with no end.
She said her own mother had sewn the pocket
out of new white linen,
and had stitched a tree on it and "Fear Not."
Grandmother Bryant had worn the pocket for fifty years.
The stitches had faded and the pocket was patched.
Still, it could hold rosemary, pennyroyal, knitbone,
linen bandages, small scissors, and two gold buttons.

Grandmother Bryant said, "Sarah, take this pocket.
Wear its old oak tree and healing plants
until I need to bandage a cut or treat a fever."

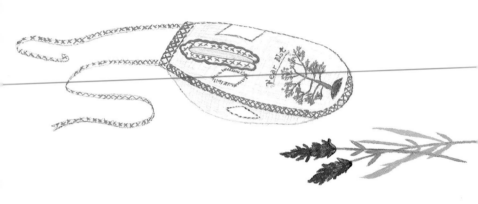

Sarah wore the pocket while they planted cabbages,
and she put it by her pillow that night.

⚜ Sarah's Days and Nights

SOME MORNINGS Sarah sat by Shoe Peg in the sunshine.
She made dolls from full-skirted hollyhocks
and watched them dance in the breeze.
Some nights she remembered the twirling, circling flames.
Then Grandmother Bryant sat by her bed
and told the story again
of her own mother stitching the pocket.
Some days Sarah washed the breakfast spoons
and gave table scraps to the one-eyed cat.

Some nights she called in her sleep for Patches
and woke up weeping.
Then Grandfather Bryant sat on her bed and
made up a song about gold buttons.

Some afternoons Sarah picked twigs and dirt
from woolen fleeces
and rolled catnip and small wool scraps
into a ball for the one-eyed cat.

Some nights her fingers grabbed at quilts
and she thought Grandfather's barn might burn.
But one night the ragged cat came in
and settled on her pillow.
Sarah listened to its drumlike purring
and held the soft pocket against her face.
She smelled the rosemary and not smoke.
She remembered the story and the songs.
Then she closed her eyes and dreamed of rain.

In the Bean Garden

SARAH WORE the pocket
while she worked beside her grandmother.
All morning they planted beans:
Mark a row, plant the seeds, cover the seeds.
Mark a row, plant the seeds, cover the seeds.

When they flapped their skirts
to chase Beck Chadwick's geese,
Sarah was thinking of biting, pinching beaks
and did not feel the pocket fall.

Sharp eyes saw Grandmother Bryant's pocket
at the edge of the bean garden.
Greedy hands picked it up.
"What's dropped is gone.
What's found is mine."
That afternoon
someone sold two gold buttons
to the peddler man.

SARAH LOOKED under the table, beside the benches,
by the new-planted beans, and beside the fence.
She wanted to search all night.
"I never should have worn that pocket," she said,
"but it was soft and strong."

Grandmother Bryant looked under the table,
beside the benches,
by the new-planted beans, and beside the fence.
"It was right to give Sarah the pocket—
whether it's lost or found."
Shoe Peg looked under the table, beside the benches,
by the new-planted beans, and beside the fence.
"Someone has spied and stolen it.
If it were here we would find it."

At last Sarah said,
"I will stitch a new pocket,
 with a rose and 'Fear Not.'
 I can find pennyroyal and rosemary,
 but I have no scissors and no gold buttons."

✿ Looking for Pennyroyal

ONE MORNING
Grandmother Bryant, Sarah, and the one-eyed cat
went walking to gather pennyroyal.
They found Beck Chadwick crumpled on the ground.
"I fell onto a sharp stick," she said.
Grandmother Bryant said,
"I have linen bandages and knitbone
but no scissors to cut away your stocking.
They are lost with my old pocket."
Beck Chadwick sighed and groaned as the healer worked.
Then she whispered,
"In my kitchen, in the candle box under the bench,
you'll find the pocket."

Grandmother Bryant said, "Sarah, get the pocket."
"I can't," said Sarah. "The geese."
"Take this walking stick, Sarah. Go quickly."

Sarah ran down the road, the one-eyed cat beside her.
Sarah's heart thumped like a crow caught in her chest.
She did not hear the robins or see the dandelion blossoms.
Sarah and the cat neared Beck Chadwick's house,
and the geese began to hiss.

Sarah swung the walking stick.
The one-eyed cat screamed and leapt at the geese.
They scattered to the garden.
Sarah ran into the house, found the pocket,

and went out again, holding the stick, waiting for the geese.
They grumbled and hissed, but did not come close.
Sarah and the cat ran to Grandmother Bryant.
Robins sang, "Cure him, cure him. Give him physic."

❧ Linen and Knitbone Do What They Can

GRANDMOTHER BRYANT cut away Beck Chadwick's stocking
and bandaged her leg,
and said Shoe Peg would do her farm chores
until the wound was healed.
After a few weeks Beck Chadwick was up—
as sour and grumbling as her geese—
complaining that the bandage had been too tight,
that Shoe Peg had kicked her cow.
"Linen and knitbone can't cure a sharp tongue,"
said Shoe Peg.
Sarah found a strong stick and kept it by the door—
her own cure for the geese.

⚘ Sarah Goes Home

WHEN THE bean plants were full of blossoms,
Sarah said, "I want to go home."
Grandmother Bryant said,
"Take my old pocket with the oak tree and 'Fear Not.'
There are no gold buttons, but I will give you
chamomile, rosemary, and comfrey seeds."
Shoe Peg gave her a small wooden box
with a goose feather inside.
He said, "You'd better take the one-eyed cat.
She won't be worth two crumbs without you.
You can bring us her best kitten in the fall."

⚘　⚘　⚘

They walked to Sarah's house together—
the old man, the old woman, the girl, and the cat—
while robins sang, butterflies soared,
and yellow-flowered mulleins
danced with the summer breeze.

GRANDMOTHER BRYANT'S HERBS

CATNIP: A member of the mint family, called catnip because of cats' fondness for the leaves. Catnip leaves are sometimes made into tea.

CHAMOMILE: People still drink tea made from chamomile's cream-colored flowers. Chamomile can also be added to bath water for a soothing bath.

COMFREY: When pounded, comfrey roots give off a gluey liquid that was believed to knit broken bones back together, and so it was also called knitbone. Scientists say that comfrey contains a chemical that encourages cells to grow.

DANDELION: One of the first plants to appear after winter, it was brought to this country by early immigrants so that they could have fresh greens in the spring. The leaves contain some of the same vitamins that are in oranges, broccoli, and carrots. Roasted and ground dandelion roots were a substitute for coffee.

PENNYROYAL: Dried pennyroyal leaves were used to keep moths out of woolens and bedbugs out of sheets and quilts. The leaves were rubbed over the skin to keep insects away. Oil of pennyroyal is still used to repel insects.

ROSEMARY: The plant's needle-like leaves are used in cooking and can be made into tea. People who felt dizzy were sometimes given rosemary leaves to smell because of their strong scent.